A Change of Plans

A Change of Plans

by Alan Benjamin
illustrated by Steven Kellogg

Four Winds Press · New York

LIBRARY OF CONGRESS CATALOGING IN PUBLICATION DATA

Benjamin, Alan.   A change of plans.

   SUMMARY: When the Brown family decides to go for a boat ride and a picnic, they take along so many people that they end up having a swim and a picnic instead.
   [1. Stories in rhyme. 2. Picnicking—Fiction. 3. Family life—Fiction] I. Kellogg, Steven, ill. II. Title.
PZ8.3.B437Ch   [E]   82-1521
ISBN 0-590-07730-9   AACR2

Published by Four Winds Press. A division of Scholastic Inc., New York, N.Y.
Text copyright © 1982 by Alan Benjamin. Illustrations copyright © 1982 by Steven Kellogg.
All rights reserved. Printed in the United States of America.
Library of Congress Catalog Card Number: 82-1521
1   2   3   4   5   86   85   84   83   82

For Jesse Benjamin Hoffman.—A.B.

To Uncle Jerry and his terrific family.—S.K.

Mr. and Mrs. Bartholomew Brown
lived by a lake about five miles from town.

They had seven children, three cats, and two dogs,
a horse and a hen and a litter of hogs.
A monkey, a donkey, a skunk, and a goat,
a family of mice and an old wooden boat.

One Sunday morning when breakfast was done,
Mrs. Brown said, "Let's go out for some fun."

"I'm tired of movies," declared Mr. Brown.

"Yes," said the kids, "and the circus left town."

Mrs. Brown suggested a ride on the lake.

"That's fine," said her husband. "Now what shall we take?"

THE
JOLLY
JELLY
BEAN

JUST MARRIED

They packed three plump pies: cherry, rhubarb, and yam,
and some ham and some lamb and some strawberry jam.
And pink pickled pig's feet and popcorn and pears,
some bread and some cheese and some chocolate eclairs.

As they boarded the boat, someone said, "We can't go without Grandma and Grandpa and Aunt Sally Jo."

Then Grandma remembered Aunt Lil and Aunt Lou
and Uncle Leroy and a cousin or two.

As they started to leave, a few neighbors passed by.
"Come aboard," called the Browns. "We have plenty of pie."

They had gone a short way when their eight-year-old, Tim, said, "Wouldn't we all rather go for a swim?"

They floated and frolicked the whole afternoon,

then had a fine picnic beneath a full moon.